Elizabeth & Kate,
  with lots of love
      from Granny   September 1995
(This book won the Smartie book prize)

To Faye Theresa,
my "great" niece
T.C.

First published 1994 by
Walker Books Ltd
87 Vauxhall Walk
London SE11 5HJ

10 9 8 7 6 5 4 3 2 1

This book has been typeset in
Stempel Schneidler Medium.

Printed in Italy

British Library Cataloguing in Publication Data
A catalogue record for this book is available
from the British Library.

ISBN 0-7445-2220-X

So Much

WRITTEN BY
TRISH COOKE

ILLUSTRATED BY
HELEN OXENBURY

WALKER BOOKS

They weren't doing anything,
Mum and the baby,
nothing really...
Then,
DING DONG!
"Oooooooh!"

Mum looked at the door,
the baby looked at Mum.
It was ...

Auntie,
Auntie Bibba.
Auntie Bibba came inside with her
arms out wide, wide, wide
and one big, big smile.

"Oooooooh!" she said.
"I want to squeeze him,
I want to squeeze the baby,
I want to squeeze him
SO MUCH!"

And she sat the baby
on her knee
to play clap-clap,
stamp your foot,
then she read him a book.
"Mmmmmmm…"

They weren't doing anything,
Mum and the baby and Auntie Bibba,
nothing really…

Then,
DING DONG!
"Hello, hello!"

Mum looked at the door,
Auntie Bibba looked at the baby,
the baby looked at Mum.
It was …

Uncle,
Uncle Didi.
Uncle Didi came inside
with his eyebrows
raise high, high, high
and his lips scrunch up
small, small, small.
"Hello, hello," he said.
"I want to kiss him,
I want to kiss the baby,
I want to kiss him
SO MUCH!"

And he put the baby
on his shoulders,
and it felt shaky, shaky.
He flip-flap him over
till he nearly drop him.
"Aieeeeee!"

They weren't doing anything,
Mum and the baby and
Auntie Bibba and Uncle Didi,
nothing really…

Then,
DING DONG!
"Yoooooo hoooooo!
Yoooooo hoooooo!"

Mum looked at the door,
Uncle Didi looked at Auntie Bibba,
Auntie Bibba looked at the baby,
the baby looked at Mum.
It was …

Nannie,
Nannie and Gran-Gran.
Nannie and Gran-Gran came inside
with their handbags cock up
to one side and their brolly hook up
on their sleeve.
"Yoooooo hoooooo!
Yoooooo hoooooo!" they said.

"I want to eat him,
I want to eat the baby,
I want to eat him
SO MUCH!"

And they hug him
and they love him
and they make him
feel so cosy,
singing songs and dancing
till it was time for sleeping.
"Zzzzzzz…"

They weren't doing anything,
Mum and the baby and Auntie Bibba
and Uncle Didi and Nannie
and Gran-Gran,
nothing really…

Then,
DING DONG!
"Hey, pow, pow!"

Mum looked at the door,
Nannie looked at Gran-Gran,
Gran-Gran looked at Uncle Didi,
Uncle Didi looked at Auntie Bibba,
Auntie Bibba looked at the baby.
It was …

Cousin,
Cousin Kay-Kay (and Big Cousin Ross).
Cousin Kay-Kay came inside
and he spin up his hat
round and round
and he do like he riding horsey,
giddy-up, giddy-up.

"Hey, pow, pow!" he said.
"I want to fight him,
 I want to fight the baby,
 I want to fight him
 SO MUCH!"

And they wrestle
and they wrestle.
He push the baby first,
the baby hit him back.
He give the baby pinch,
the baby give him slap.
And then they laugh
and laugh and laugh.
"Huh huh huh!"

And the house was full, full, full,
and they sit down there
waiting for the next
DING DONG!
They wait and they wait
but it never come.
Mum said, "Is everybody all right?"
and the baby and
Cousin start to fight again,
Nannie and Gran-Gran
take out cards and dominoes,
Uncle Didi start to slap
them down on the table,
and Auntie Bibba play
some records really loud.
Mum said, "What madness all around!"

They weren't doing anything,
Mum and the baby and Auntie Bibba
and Uncle Didi and Nannie and
Gran-Gran and Cousin Kay-Kay,
nothing really…

Then,
DING DONG!

"I'm home!"
and everybody stopped.
Mum picked the baby up
and they all wait by the door…

"SURPRISE!"
everybody said,
and Mum said,
"HAPPY BIRTHDAY, DADDY!"
and everybody joined in.

Then Daddy rub the baby face
against the whiskers on his chin,
and Mum brought in the food
that she'd been cooking…

Everybody enjoyed the party.

And when it was time
for them to go
and everybody tired …
the baby wanted to play
some more.
Mum said, "No!"
She put him to bed,
but …

the baby played
bounce-bounce with Ted,
played bounce-bounce in his cot,
and he remembered
everybody saying
how they wanted
to SQUEEZE
and KISS
and EAT
and FIGHT him …

because they loved him
SO MUCH!